**W9-COI-143**

## DATE DUE

| | | | |
|---|---|---|---|
| JY 14 '92 | NOV 09 | MY 23 '03 | |
| JUL 23 | FEB 17 | AG 06 '03 | |
| AG 10 '92 | DC 01 99 | AG 11 03 | |
| | OC 11 '99 | AG 13 03 | |
| AG 14 '92 | OC 16 '0 | DE 02 00 | |
| AG 22 '9 | NO 24 99 | | |
| AG 21 '93 | MR 01 00 | | |
| SE 3 00 | MY 17 01 | | |
| OC 2 '93 | JY 16 02 | | |
| OC 30 9 | SE 20 02 | | |
| SEP 05 9 | JY 14 03 | | |
| FEB 18 9 | | | |

DEMCO

# Three Kittens

# Three Kittens

by Mirra Ginsburg

Translated from the Russian of V. Suteyev

## Pictures by Giulio Maestro

Crown Publishers, Inc., New York

Published by Crown Publishers, Inc., 225 Park Avenue South, New York,
10003 and represented in Canada by the Canadian MANDA Group
CROWN is a trademark of Crown Publishers, Inc.
Manufactured in Hong Kong by South China Printing Co.
Library of Congress Catalog Card Number: 72-92383
10   9   8   7   6

ISBN 0-517-50328-X
      0-517-56551-X (paperback)

# Three Kittens

# Three kittens—black, gray, and white—

saw a mouse...

and ran after it.

The mouse jumped into
a can of flour.

The kittens jumped in after it.

The mouse ran away,

and three white kittens
           climbed out of the can.

Three white kittens
        saw a toad in the yard,

and dashed after it.

The toad jumped into
        an old stovepipe.

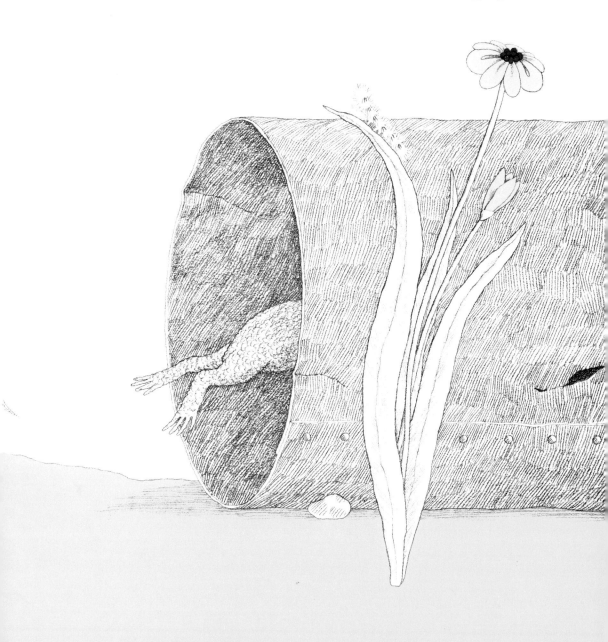

The kittens crawled in after it.

The toad hopped away...

and three black kittens
          crawled out of the pipe.

Three black kittens
    saw a fish in the pond...

and dove in after it.

The fish swam away...

and three wet kittens
came up from the pond.

Three wet kittens went home.

On the way they dried out...

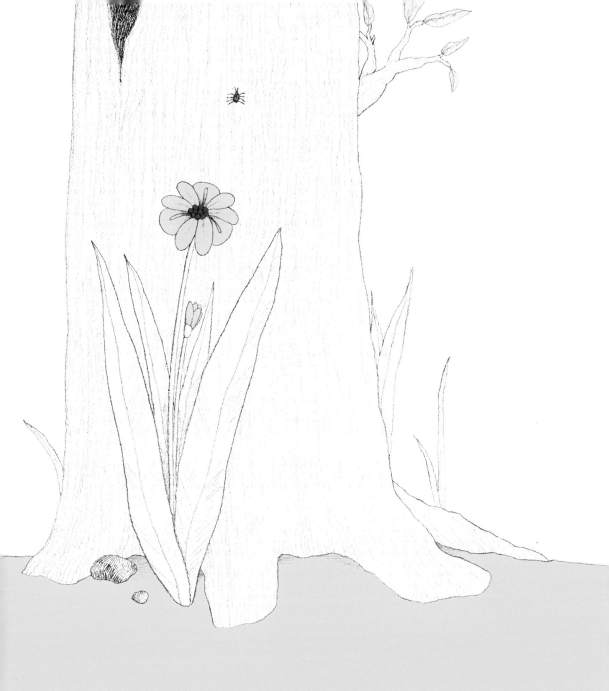

and became as before–

black, gray, and white.